Making a Whole Person

Traditional Inuit Education

Qinuisaarniq ("resiliency") is a program created to educate Nunavummiut and all Canadians about the history and impacts of residential schools, policies of assimilation, and other colonial acts that affected the Canadian Arctic.

Published in Canada by Arvaaq Press Inc. | www.arvaaq.com

Arvaaq Press Inc.
(Iqaluit) 2434 Paurngaq Crescent, Iqaluit, Nunavut, X0A 2H0
(Toronto) 614 Mount Pleasant Road, Unit 1, Toronto, Ontario, M4S 2M8

Printed in Canada.

Library and Archives Canada Cataloguing in Publication

Title: Making a whole person : traditional Inuit education / written by Monica Ittusardjuat ; illustrated by Yong Ling Kang.
Names: Ittusardjuat, Monica, author. | Kang, Yong Ling, illustrator.
Identifiers: Canadiana 20190215941 | ISBN 9781774502051 (hardcover)
Subjects: LCSH: Inuit—Education—Canada—Juvenile literature. | LCSH: Inuit—Social life and customs—Juvenile literature. | LCSH: Experiential learning—Canada—Juvenile literature. | LCSH: Ethnoscience—Canada—Juvenile literature.
Classification: LCC E99.E7 I88 2020 | DDC j371.829/9712071—dc23

ISBN: 978-1-77450-205-1

Making a Whole Person

Traditional Inuit Education

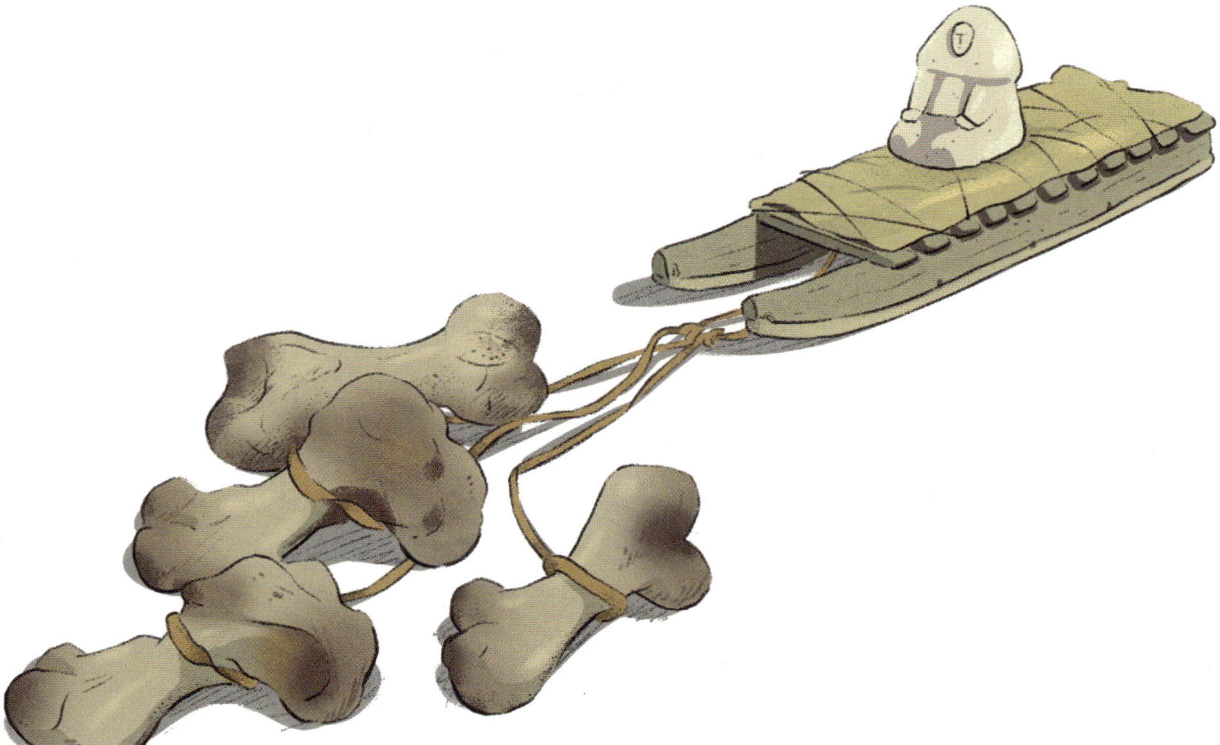

WRITTEN BY

Monica Ittusardjuat

ILLUSTRATED BY

Yong Ling Kang

Before schools were introduced to the Inuit, we were taught by our relatives.

Our family members taught us by showing us how to do something and explaining the steps. Then they would tell us to try it ourselves. We also learned by playing games.

We lived in a *qarmaq* (sod house) in the winter. One of the games we used to play was Uat Tamanna. This was how our relatives taught us the different parts of the qarmaq. They would blindfold us and we would point, saying, "*Uat tamanna* (this is the wall), *aki tamanna* (this is the pantry), *igliq tamanna* (this is the bed platform), *qariaq tamanna* (this is the extra bed), ummm...." Then they would rotate us and we would try to touch someone. The other players would quietly try to get away. Whoever got touched would be the next one to be blindfolded.

Another game we used to play was Hide the Thimble. One kid would hide a thimble while the other kids kept their heads down. You were not allowed to hide the thimble inside or behind something—you had to put it somewhere it could be seen. The first person to find it would be the next one to have a turn hiding it. This game taught us how to be alert and taught us hunting skills. We had to be able to identify, for example, a white animal on the snow, which can be hard to find even if it's not hiding.

Our qarmaq used to be pasted with pages from magazines to brighten up the home. When we were in bed, we used to play Hand and Pull, where we tried to find as many capital letter *H*'s as we could in the pages. We did the same with trying to find the letter *s*, which looked like a snake. We were taught this game because we had to do a lot of searching on the land when we went hunting.

H

We also played I'm Thinking Of.... This was a riddle game. My favourite was, "I'm thinking of something that has an eye but cannot see." The other kids would try to guess what you were thinking of. If someone guessed right, then it would be their turn. Sometimes we would fall asleep playing that game. Another game we played often was trying to get your siblings to guess which family you were thinking of by saying something like, "Father, mother, son, daughter." These games exercised our brains and made us stretch our minds.

I was also taught string games. I learned many string games, and I could even sing or chant the poems that come with some of the figures. The string games helped me learn to flex my fingers so that I could work with my hands, especially for sewing, and to remember stories.

We used to "play real" everything that the adults did. My father made me a family of wooden dolls. There was a mother, a father, a daughter, and a son. My mother would cut out patterns for their clothing and she would teach me how to sew them together. She showed me how to make an *amauti* and women's pants. When I got stuck, she would take the sewing, show me how to do it, and then give it back to me and let me try again. If my stitches were not satisfactory to her, she would undo them and show me how to do it better. Then she would give it back to me to continue from where she left off.

Little boys used to have toy dog teams, just like their fathers. They used the femur bones of a seal as the dogs, and they were harnessed like real dogs. Their fathers helped them make the harness. They would put a lemming skin on the toy *qamutiik*, the way the adults put caribou skins on their qamutiik. Then they would pretend to mush their dogs just like their fathers, saying “left,” “right,” and “hurry up.”

Little boys were taught how to check the ice with a harpoon at the floe edge to see if it was safe. Before they were taught how to harpoon an animal, they were taught where to hit the animal to kill it. They were taught which animals to harpoon in the heart, which animals to harpoon in the head, and which animals to maim and then kill when it was the right time. They were taught how to butcher each animal for different purposes.

Boys would come along with their male relatives on hunting trips at first, just to watch and learn. When a boy's father decided it was the right time he would guide his son along. The most important thing they were taught was to respect the animals and not to hurt them as a game, but only to kill them for food and clothing and other things we needed. They were taught to only kill as many animals as they needed to eat.

It was important for both boys and girls to learn about sharing. When a boy caught his first animal, the first choices of meat would be given to the midwife who helped at his birth, to his grandparents, and to the relatives of his namesake. Every piece of meat was shared. The skin would be dried and given away or sold. If it was sold, the parents would buy some treats and invite everyone for a candy toss. Little girls were taught to give their first pair of mitts or *kamiik* to someone they respected. This was so that she would want to keep sewing and make more clothing to share.

We were taught cultural and traditional values by example, through trial and error. My mother would visit Elders with me. She told me I didn't need to do or say anything, but just go and see them. They might need someone to help them fetch water or take out the garbage or do other chores. We were taught to respect and honour Elders.

Inuit taught their children about weather, hand games for coordination and flexibility, and songs and legends to teach about values and what not to do. It was all about showing, telling, trial and error, practice, experience, watching, listening, and using all your senses.

I once heard an Elder talk about traditional education as being *inunnguqsainiq*, which literally means "making a human being." He talked about one man who knew what to do in every situation. All his senses were so fine tuned, he was like a shaman, although he wasn't one. This was an example of someone who was well educated: someone who knew how to use all his senses, to the point of almost having a sixth sense.

We were taught not to boast or boss people around. We were taught not to be prideful or show off, but always to share. You had to take on responsibility and be accountable for your actions and look out for one another. We were taught to try and have more than enough, in case someone else might need something. Everything was done for the good of everyone, and you had to do your part, no matter how small.

Glossary and Pronunciation Guide

Notes on Inuktitut pronunciation: There are some sounds in Inuktitut that may be unfamiliar to English speakers. The pronunciations below convey those sounds in the following ways:

- A double vowel (for example, *aa*, *ee*) creates a long vowel sound.
- Capitalized letters indicate the emphasis.
- **q** is a "uvular" sound, which is a sound that comes from the very back of the throat (the uvula). This is different from the **k** sound, which is the same as the typical English **k** sound.
- **R** is a rolled "r" sound.

For more Inuktitut and Inuinnaqtun pronunciation resources, please visit inhabiteducation.com/inuitnipingit.

qarmaq (QAR-maq): a sod house; a dwelling Inuit lived in during the fall and winter. Traditionally, the frames were made of bowhead whale bones.

uat (U-at): wall.

aki (A-ki): pantry.

igliq (IG-liq): bed.

amauti (a-MOW-ti): a woman's parka with a large hood, made for carrying a baby.

qamutiik (qa-mu-TEEK): a sled. Inuit used qamutiit pulled by dogs for hunting and travelling in the winter.

kamiik (ka-MEEK): two skin boots.

inunnguqsainiq (I-nu-nnguq-sa-i-niq): a word to describe traditional Inuit education; literally "making a human being."

About the Author

Monica Ittusardjuat was taken from her parents and sent to residential school at the age of seven, at a time when Inuit lived a subsistence way of life in winter camps and roamed around in spring and summer, following animals when they were plentiful. She went to three residential schools: Chesterfield Inlet, NWT (now Nunavut), for primary school; Churchill, Manitoba, for junior high; and St. Norbert, Manitoba, for high school.

Monica graduated from McGill University in 1987. While teaching Community NTEP (Nunavut Teacher Education Program) in Nunavut, she earned her M.Ed. through the University of Prince Edward Island. She was the honour student for Baffin Island. She taught for many years in elementary schools, high schools, and the Nunavut Teacher Education Program, as well as in the Interpreter/Translator Program at Nunavut Arctic College.

Monica tried to retire at the age of 60, but the habit of going to work was hard to break. She was the National Inuit Language Coordinator at Inuit Tapiriit Kanatami from 2016 to 2018 and is now Senior Inuktitut Editor at Inhabit Education, which she describes as her dream job.

About the Illustrator

Yong Ling is an illustrator and avid comic book reader living in Toronto. She is inspired by simple, day-to-day experiences and her nostalgia of childhood. She suspects that her fondness of drawing may be caused by watching too many cartoons. Raised in tropical Singapore, she enjoys slow water sports and spicy food.

Historical Note

For over a century, beginning in the mid-1800s and continuing into the late 1990s, Indigenous children in Canada were taken from their homes and communities and placed in institutions called "Indian residential schools." While residential schools had existed in Canada since 1831, it was not until the 1950s that a significant number of these schools were operating in the Canadian North. By 1964, over three-quarters of school-aged Inuit children were attending residential school.

Qinuisaarniq ("resiliency") is a program created to educate Nunavummiu about the history and impacts of residential schools, policies of assimilation, and other colonial acts that affected the Canadian Arctic. The resources in this program include personal interviews, testimony, anc writing; non-fiction informational resources; and information about life in the North before colonialism.

For a complete list of resources, visit www.inhabiteducation.com.